Dear Parent:
Your child's love of reading starts here!

Every child learns to read in a different way and at his or her own speed. Some go back and forth between reading levels and read favorite books again and again. Others read through each level in order. You can help your young reader improve and become more confident by encouraging his or her own interests and abilities. From books your child reads with you to the first books he or she reads alone, there are I Can Read Books for every stage of reading:

SHARED READING
Basic language, word repetition, and whimsical illustrations, ideal for sharing with your emergent reader

BEGINNING READING
Short sentences, familiar words, and simple concepts for children eager to read on their own

2

READING WITH HELP
Engaging stories, longer sentences, and language play for developing readers

3

READING ALONE
Complex plots, challenging vocabulary, and high-interest topics for the independent reader

4

ADVANCED READING
Short paragraphs, chapters, and exciting themes for the perfect bridge to chapter books

I Can Read Books have introduced children to the joy of reading since 1957. Featuring award-winning authors and illustrators and a fabulous cast of beloved characters, I Can Read Books set the standard for beginning readers.

A lifetime of discovery begins with the magical words **"I Can Read!"**

Visit www.icanread.com for information on enriching your child's reading experience.

Transformers: Hunt for the Decepticons: Ratchet to the Rescue
 For information address HarperCollins Children's Books, a division of HarperCollins Publishers, 10 East 53rd Street, New York, NY 10022.
www.icanread.com

Library of Congress catalog card number: 2010921892
ISBN 978-0-06-199173-8
Typography by John Sazaklis

10 11 12 13 14 LP/WOR 10 9 8 7 6 5 4 3 2 1 ❖ First Edition

TRANSFORMERS

Ratchet to the Rescue

Adapted by Jennifer Frantz
Illustrated by Guido Guidi

HARPER
An Imprint of HarperCollinsPublishers

WEEEE-OOH!

WEEEE-OOH!

From nowhere, sirens blare.

An emergency vehicle
speeds onto the scene
and busts through a barrier.

But this is no ordinary emergency,
and this is no ordinary vehicle.
It's RATCHET,
the Autobot medic!
In a flash, Ratchet switches
from a rescue truck
into an awesome Autobot.

Now it's time to save his friends
Sideswipe and Bumblebee.
These banged up 'bots
have had a nasty run-in
with some evil Decepticons.
Ratchet quickly gets to work,
sawing through a metal bar
to free Bumblebee.

Next, he scans Sideswipe with his laser scanner to see what's wrong.

“Hold tight,” Ratchet tells his fellow ’bot. “I can fix you.” And he does.

Ratchet can fix almost anything or anyone.
His motto is, "If you can break it,
I can remake it."

Ratchet is a smart 'bot
with a clever mind.
Back on Cybertron,
the Autobots' planet,
he was a doctor.
Ratchet loved to tinker with machines
and learned everything
there was to know
about making and fixing their parts.

This old Autobot
has seen many battles
and lost many friends.

Through the years, and the battles,
Ratchet has grown tougher and tougher.
But his inner spark still shines
strong and true.

Ratchet is always there
for his fellow Autobots.

Just ask his friends
Ironhide, Sideswipe,
and Bumblebee.

With his strong senses,
Ratchet can warn the other Autobots
when trouble is coming.
"Look out!"

Ratchet doesn’t like to fight
unless it is necessary.
But in a battle he’s a ’bot
you want on your side.
“Ironhide, I’ve got your back!”

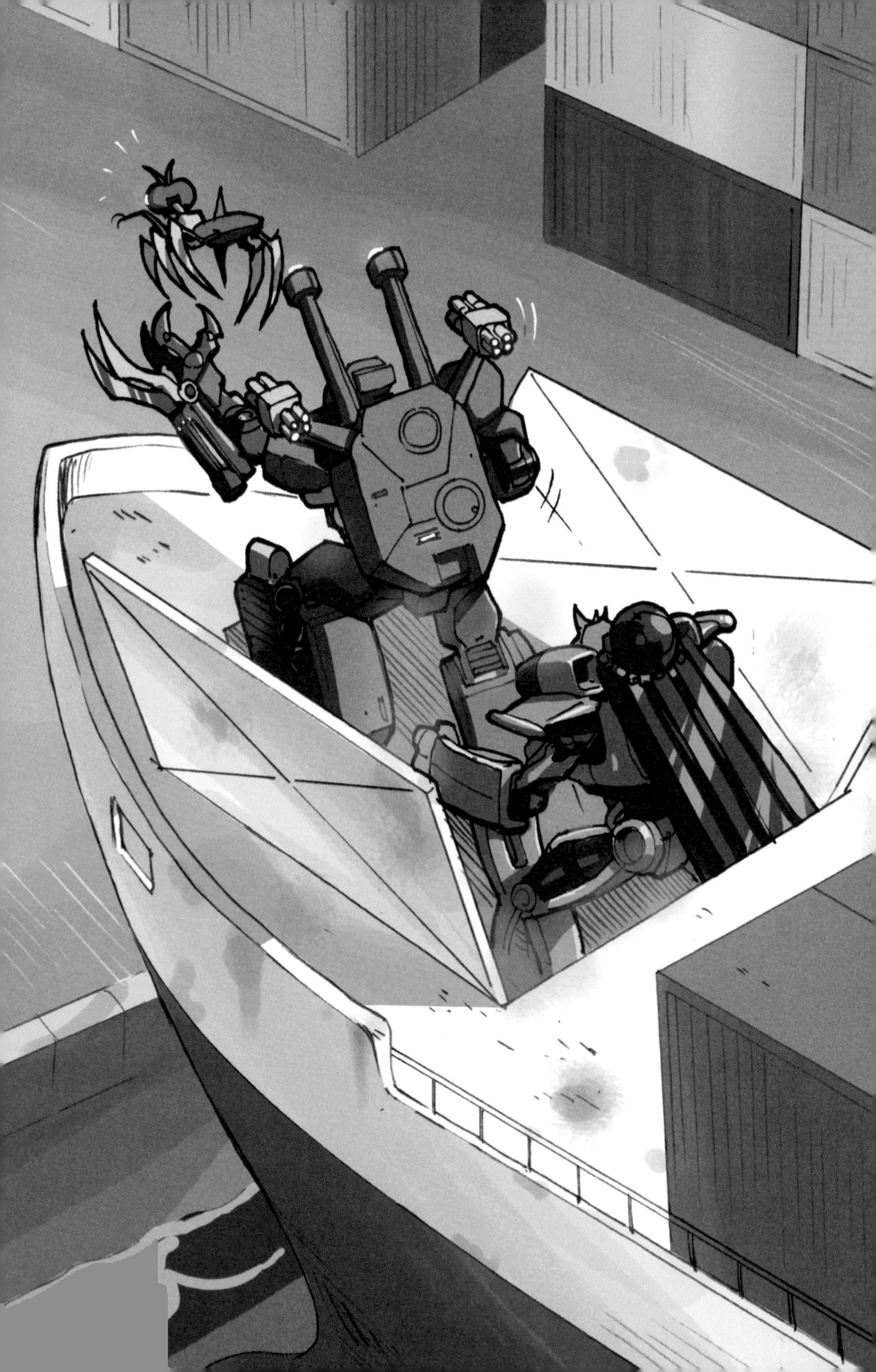

Ratchet doesn't just help
injured Autobots.
He can also hold his own
against Decepticon enemies.
WHAM!
Ratchet blasts two Decepticons,
Brawl and Blackout.
He holds them off
until his Autobot friends
can safely escape.

Ratchet is a ’bot bound by honor and a sense of duty.

He will fight until the end alongside
the Autobots' fearless leader,
Optimus Prime.
Any time . . .
Any place . . .

Together with the other Autobots,
Ratchet defends the Earth
and the universe
from the evil Decepticons
and their leader Megatron.

But no matter how tough things get, Ratchet will always come to the rescue of a fallen friend.

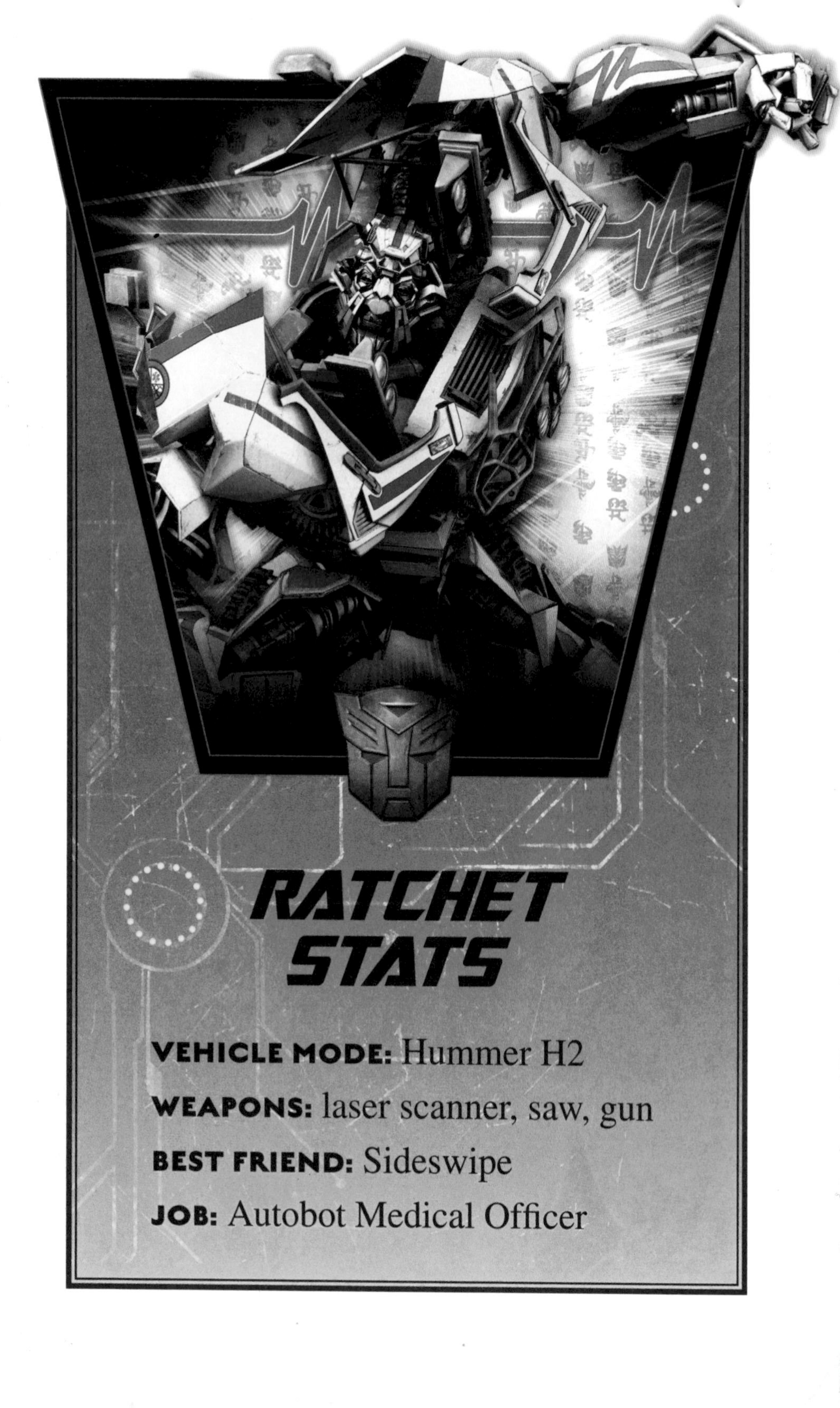
RATCHET STATS
VEHICLE MODE: Hummer H2
WEAPONS: laser scanner, saw, gun
BEST FRIEND: Sideswipe
JOB: Autobot Medical Officer